S0-CMS-437

Pebble®

First Biographies
Betsy Ross

by Jan Mader

Consulting Editor: Gail Saunders-Smith, PhD

Consultant: National Flag Foundation
Pittsburgh, Pennsylvania

Capstone
press®
Mankato, Minnesota

92 R

Pebble Books are published by Capstone Press,
151 Good Counsel Drive, P.O. Box 669, Mankato, Minnesota 56002.
www.capstonepress.com

1 2 3 4 5 6 12 11 10 09 08 07

Library of Congress Cataloging-in-Publication Data
Mader, Jan.
    Betsy Ross / by Jan Mader.
    p. cm. —(Pebble Books. First biographies)
    Summary: "Simple text and photographs present the life and legend of Betsy
Ross"—Provided by publisher.
    Includes bibliographical references and index.
    ISBN-13: 978-0-7368-6702-3 (hardcover)
    ISBN-10: 0-7368-6702-3 (hardcover)
    ISBN-13: 978-0-7368-7842-5 (softcover)
    ISBN-10: 0-7368-7842-4 (softcover)
    1. Ross, Betsy, 1752–1836—Juvenile literature. 2. Revolutionaries—United
States—Biography—Juvenile literature. 3. Women revolutionaries—United
States—Biography—Juvenile literature. 4. United States—History—Revolution,
1775–1783—Flags—Juvenile literature. 5. Flags—United States—History—18th
century—Juvenile literature. I. Title. II. Series.
E302.6.R77M33 2007
973.3092—dc22   2006020930

Note to Parents and Teachers

The First Biographies set supports national history standards for
units on people and culture. This book describes and illustrates
the life of Betsy Ross. The images support early readers in
understanding the text. The repetition of words and phrases helps
early readers learn new words. This book also introduces early
readers to subject-specific vocabulary words, which are defined
in the Glossary section. Early readers may need assistance to read
some words and to use the Table of Contents, Glossary, Read More,
Internet Sites, and Index sections of the book.

Table of Contents

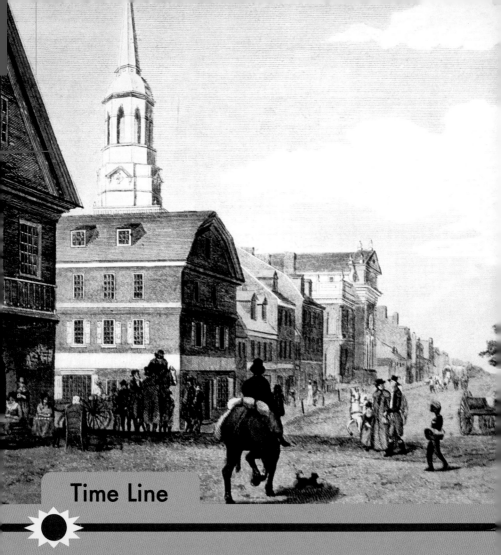

Time Line

1752
born

Early Years

Elizabeth Griscom
was born in 1752
in Philadelphia.
She had many brothers
and sisters. Elizabeth's
nickname was Betsy.

 a street in Philadelphia near Betsy's home

Time Line

1752
born

1758
learns to sew

6

Betsy went to
a Quaker school
when she was six.
She learned reading, math,
and how to sew.
Betsy liked to sew.

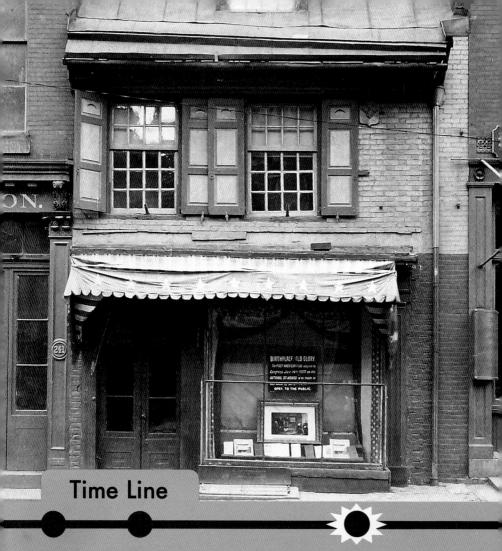

Time Line

1752
born

1758
learns to sew

1773
gets married;
opens shop

8

Betsy's parents wanted her
to learn a trade.
So Betsy worked
at a sewing shop.
Then Betsy met John Ross.
They married in 1773 and
opened a new shop together.

 Betsy's house and shop in 1890

Time Line

1752
born

1758
learns to sew

1773
gets married;
opens shop

John died in 1776.
Betsy ran the shop
by herself.
She made clothing,
furniture covers, and flags.

Time Line

1752
born

1758
learns to sew

1773
gets married;
opens shop

The First Flag

At the time,
the United States of America
was a new country.
It needed a flag.
Legend says that Betsy sewed
the first American flag.

Time Line

1752
born

1758
learns to sew

1773
gets married;
opens shop

The flag was red,
white, and blue.
It had 13 stars
and 13 stripes.
In 1777, it became
America's official flag.

1777
The Stars and Stripes
becomes America's flag

Time Line

1752	1758		1773
born	learns to sew		gets married; opens shop

Later Years

Later, Betsy married
two more times.
She had seven daughters
and many grandchildren.
Her family liked to listen
to stories about Betsy's life.

1777
The Stars and Stripes
becomes America's flag

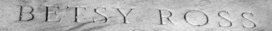

Time Line

1752
born

1758
learns to sew

1773
gets married;
opens shop

Betsy died in 1836.
Her grandson William
told the story
of Betsy making
the first American flag.

Betsy's grave

1777
The Stars and Stripes
becomes America's flag

1836
dies

Time Line

1752
born

1758
learns to sew

1773
gets married;
opens shop

Symbol of America

Today, no one is sure
if Betsy really made
the first flag.
But, like the flag, Betsy Ross
is still a symbol of America.

1777
The Stars and Stripes
becomes America's flag

1836
dies

Glossary

legend—a story passed down from earlier times; it is hard to prove if legends are true.

nickname—a name used instead of a person's real name

official—approved by a group or someone in charge

Quaker—a religious group also called the Society of Friends

symbol—a person or object that reminds people of something else; the story of Betsy Ross reminds people of America's first flag.

trade—a job that requires training

Read More

Cox, Vicki. *Betsy Ross: A Flag for a New Nation.* Leaders of the American Revolution. Philadelphia: Chelsea House, 2006.

Dahl, Michael. *Keep on Sewing, Betsy Ross!: A Fun Song About the First American Flag.* Minneapolis: Picture Window Books, 2004.

Silate, Jennifer. *The American Flag.* Primary Sources of American Symbols. New York: PowerKids, 2006.

Internet Sites

FactHound offers a safe, fun way to find Internet sites related to this book. All of the sites on FactHound have been researched by our staff.

Here's how:

1. Visit *www.facthound.com*

2. Choose your grade level.

3. Type in this book ID **0736867023** for age-appropriate sites. You may also browse subjects by clicking on letters, or by clicking on pictures and words.

4. Click on the **Fetch It** button.

FactHound will fetch the best sites for you!

Index

Word Count: 197
Grades: 1–2
Early-Intervention Level: 24

Editorial Credits

Sarah L. Schuette, editor; Mary Bode, book designer; Wanda Winch,
    photo researcher/photo editor

Photo Credits

Getty Images Inc./Hulton Archive/Painting by Lambert, 20
The Granger Collection, New York, 8, 10, 12
Mary Evans Picture Library, 16
North Wind Picture Archives, 6, 14
Peter Newark's Pictures, 4
SuperStock, cover, 1
www.thecemeteryproject.com/Michael Reed, 18